Tom the Naughty Tooth Fairy

by Elizabeth Dale and Adriana Puglisi

FRANKLIN WATTS
LONDON•SYDNEY

Tom was a tooth fairy.

He had a very important job.

Every night, he flew to children's houses.

He collected teeth

from under the children's pillows.

Then he gave them a coin

for each tooth.

But sometimes Tom played with
the children's toys, too.

One night, Tom flew into Polly's room.

It was full of lovely toys to play with!

He played with the teddies,

stroking their fur.

He rocked on the rocking horse

and played with the toy train.

Then Tom saw the dolls house.

He flew in to say 'hello' to the dolls.

He ran up and down the tiny stairs.

He sat at the table

and poured tea into the tiny cups.

Suddenly, Polly's alarm clock went off.
She started to wake up.

"Oh no! It's six o'clock," said Tom.
"I have to go!"

He ran to the window and flew out,
just in time.

But he had forgotten to collect

Polly's tooth.

Tom flew back to Fairyland
as fast as he could.

"You are late," said the Fairy Boss.
"Did you get lost?"

"I'm sorry," said Tom. "I was playing with Polly's toys, and I forgot the time."

"Oh, Tom, not again! You are naughty," said the Fairy Boss.

"Go and put Polly's tooth with the rest."

Tom felt in his bag for the tooth.

Oh no! He had forgotten it!

Polly would be so sad.

He would have to go back.

That night, after it was dark,

Tom set off.

He made sure Polly was asleep

and flew into her room.

He didn't look at the toys.

He didn't stop to play.

He had to get Polly's tooth.

He crept over to the bed,

and slid his hand under her pillow.

Yes! The tooth was still there!

Slowly, Tom pulled the tooth out

and put it in his bag.

Then he put a shiny coin
where the tooth had been.

Tom flew off into the night.

He had lots more work to do.

When Polly woke up in the morning,

she felt under her pillow.

There, where the tooth had been,

was a bright shiny coin!

The tooth fairy had come at last!

Story order

Look at these 5 pictures and captions.
Put the pictures in the right order
to retell the story.

1

Tom is in trouble with the Fairy Boss.

2

Tom returns to collect the tooth.

3

Tom has a lot more work to do.

4

Tom is busy playing with the toys.

5

Polly will be upset she has no coin.

Guide for Independent Reading

This series is designed to provide an opportunity for your child to read on their own. These notes are written for you to help your child choose a book and to read it independently.

In school, your child's teacher will often be using reading books which have been banded to support the process of learning to read. Use the book band colour your child is reading in school to help you make a good choice. *Tom the Naughty Tooth Fairy* is a good choice for children reading at Turquoise Band in their classroom to read independently. The aim of independent reading is to read this book with ease, so that your child enjoys the story and relates it to their own experiences.

About the book
Tom is a busy tooth fairy. Sometimes he forgets to collect the teeth from children's pillows, and plays with their toys instead. But the Fairy Boss soon reminds Tom what he is supposed to do!

Before reading
Help your child to learn how to make good choices by asking:
"Why did you choose this book? Why do you think you will enjoy it?"
Look at the cover together and ask: "What do you think the story will be about?" Ask your child to think of what they already know about the story context. Then ask your child to read the title aloud. Ask: "What is Tom's job? What does he have to do to be a good tooth fairy?"
Remind your child that they can sound out the letters to make a word if they get stuck.
Decide together whether your child will read the story independently or read it aloud to you.

During reading

Remind your child of what they know and what they can do independently. If reading aloud, support your child if they hesitate or ask for help by telling the word. If reading to themselves, remind your child that they can come and ask for your help if stuck.

After reading

Support comprehension by asking your child to tell you about the story. Use the story order puzzle to encourage your child to retell the story in the right sequence, in their own words. The correct sequence can be found on the next page.

Help your child think about the messages in the book that go beyond the story and ask: "Do you think Tom has a difficult job?" Give your child a chance to respond to the story: "Did you have a favourite part? What would you have done if you were Tom?"

Extending learning

Help your child understand the story structure by using the same sentence patterning and adding different elements. "Let's make up a new story about elves. They are busy helping Santa wrap presents for children, but one gets distracted and plays with the toys instead of wrapping them. What might happen next?"

In the classroom, your child's teacher may be teaching examples of descriptive language such as expressions about time. Locate the phrases relating to time in the story (such as 'one night', 'that night' or 'in the morning'). Ask your child to find as many as they can, and then think of some more examples.

Franklin Watts
First published in Great Britain in 2018
by The Watts Publishing Group

Copyright © The Watts Publishing Group 2018

Series Editors: Jackie Hamley and Melanie Palmer
Series Advisors: Dr Sue Bodman and Glen Franklin
Series Designer: Peter Scoulding

A CIP catalogue record for this book is
available from the British Library.

ISBN 978 1 4451 6209 6 (hbk)
ISBN 978 1 4451 6210 2 (pbk)
ISBN 978 1 4451 6211 9 (library ebook)

Printed in China

Franklin Watts
An imprint of
Hachette Children's Group
Part of The Watts Publishing Group
Carmelite House
50 Victoria Embankment
London EC4Y 0DZ

An Hachette UK Company
www.hachette.co.uk

www.franklinwatts.co.uk

Answer to Story order: 4, 1, 5, 2, 3